BEAR

LEARNS TO SHARE

Will my children, Harrison and Hailey,
share this dedication?
Yes.
— H.L.

ISBN 978-1-338-84930-1
10 9 8 7 6 5 4 3 2 1   23 24 25 26 27
Printed in the U.S.A.   40
This edition first printing, 2023

BEAR
LEARNS TO SHARE

by Hilary Leung

Scholastic Inc.

Bear has a lot to give...

...but will she share?

Will Bear share her book?

Yes.

Will she share her toothbrush?

NO! Toothbrushes are
not for sharing.

Will Bear share
her favorite toy?

Yes.

Will she share
her umbrella?

Oh yes!

Will Bear share her ice cream?

No.

Uh-oh.

Will Ladybug share her berry cake?

Yes.

What do *you* share?